# Tales from Frewyn:

## The Opera

&

## The Reporter from

## Marridon

# Tales from Frewyn:

# The Opera

## &

# The Reporter from Marridon

A Haanta Series Novella
By Michelle Franklin
Art by Twisk

*To Luis*
*For putting up with me*

# Table of Contents

## The Opera

## The Reporter from Marridon

Tales from Frewyn:
# The Opera

TWO HEARTS
TWO WARRING
NATIONS
ONE FORBIDDEN
LOVE

*Michelle Franklin*

# INTRODUCTION

The Haanta Series went on tour in September 2011. To spread word of the tour, I was advised to announce the event through a series of ads taken on various fantasy and romance websites. I thought this would be easily done, but when I was asked to write a tagline for one of the ads on an extremely popular romance blog, I had little idea what to write that would appeal to the site's general audience. I perused the various other ads on the home page and cringed to myself to see their cinema-esque taglines. I thought to myself, "Well, if I must," and proceeded to write the phrase: Two hearts, two warring nations, one forbidden love. I laughed for a good ten minutes at how ridiculous that sounded, and when I showed the ad to Twisk, she instantly went to work in drawing a picture for such a phrase. She then entreated me to write a story that would match, and therefore here it is.

# CHAPTER ONE
# THE ROYAL THEATRE

Beyond the main portion of the Diras castle keep, between the memorial garden dedicated to the kings and queens of Frewyn's past, and the latrine tower, a place where everyone in the keep must visit but where no one wished to venture, was the Royal Theatre. It was called royal due to its origin in being constructed for the enlivenment and entertainment of the king and Frewyn nobility, but over the many years of its various exhibitions and staged depictions, with the declining gradations of quality in the performances and the diminishment of the general interest thereof, the theatre was opened to the Frewyn public for proper scrutiny, gapes, and disparagement as the situation would allow. Grand balls in the royal parlour and private concerts became the amusement of choice for the Frewyn royals, and though the king still must sponsor the Frewyn Players to tender affordable evening entertainment to the rest of his kingdom, while the productions were well executed, the originality and creativity of their displays soon waned. Old favourites such as One Man's Woe and Mad Queen Maeve, the grandiose and colourful retellings of the more tragic moments in Frewyn's history, prevailed and became traditions for the various seasons the theatre underwent, but to end the monotony of reiterating the same lines and singing the same songs, a new play was often introduced on the off-season, usually written by one of the cast with the hopes of such a production becoming a fever among the people of Frewyn as the others had done.

Many attempts were made to capture the delights of the theatre-goers in this style and many times the players failed. The yeomanry, tradesmen, and artisans of the kingdom who were in want of a little evening entertainment at the end of the day were simply too well-versed in the arts and had too estimable an appreciation of writing, acting, and singing to be diverted by modest endeavors. They must have more for their hard-earned wages: they must have the pinnacle of performing arts, for they were not simple creature to be easily deceived by moderacy. Farmers left their seats and went outside to enjoy their pipes and good banter on the subjects of crop rotation and field mice; children fussed and fidgeted about, taking more pleasure in trying to step upon their friends' toes than they could derive from watching the performance; women knitted and took to carpet work while discussing and comparing the various accomplishments of their children; babes cried and were fed, and the general disinclination of the audience to attend the given piece made the actors anxious to continue. Traditional plays were one thing, but new stories that the hale and hearty Frewyn spectators did not enjoy were entirely another. The distress and vexation the actors felt was expatiated by the audience's unwillingness to regard them, and though Frewyns were never uncivil at first, tedium accorded was deserving of retaliation. Word soon reached the rest of the capital of the paltry attempts to entertain. A full theatre was reduced to half, the players grew despondent, and from their desperation to be adored, and from their worry of King Alasdair reneging his sponsorship, a new production of Mad Queen Maeve was staged and all good Frewyn society was disposed to return to their seats and marvel at the performance.

Though the desires of the audience had been appeased, proven by their standing ovations and the increase in ticket sales, the aspirations of the Frewyn Players to perform something new and inspiring were yet unfounded. Everything that could be done to secure their livelihoods was done, but everything that could be done to secure their happiness and fulfillment was not. They pined for new lines, new characters and new choreography, and their only reprieve from the glaring uniformity came in concerts and festivities for the Frewyn holidays. A concert or two was given by the majesties to exercise their musical talents, the ballet of Sesterna made its annual visit, the acrobats from Lucentia came but twice a year when the weather suited their northern constitutions, and though these displays were enjoyed by the audience and therefore envied by the Frewyn Players, none besieged and confounded them all so well as the Marridon Opera. With voices so strident, subjects so catastrophic, costumes so outlandish and sets so refined, the opera more astounded than delighted. The Frewyn audience applauded because they knew they must to give propriety to their guests where it was due, but the amount of pleasure derived from such a performance was left to be guessed by each. Their general perplexity was mistaken for complete awe: the indiscernible feelings, the halfhearted accolades, the talk of not knowing what to make of such glorified tragedy was enough to convince the players of the opera's magnificence. Only something so brilliantly contrived could amaze to such a degree, and the more it stunned, the more Frewyn should flock to it in hopes of understanding it.

A Frewyn opera was therefore to be performed, and the subject of the recital must be one to which every Frewyn could relate: it must have love, it must have war, it must have loss and sanguinary themes, but above all it must be familiar. The Galleisian War was talked of and songs were even written to address such content, but while there was a certain romance in battle for those who had never fought one, there was even more romance to be found in another quarter: the heroes of war, their conflicts and tribulations, their joys and triumphs were where true character could be discovered, for they must have their tales told and glorified, and two such Frewyn heroes would be the very question to draw all of Frewyn to the theatre once more.

# Chapter Two
## The Announcement

The placards and posters announcing Mad Queen Maeve's tenth iteration were taken away and another announcement was set in its place, one for a new play of certain distinction, whose book was written by Frewyn's champion auteur and whose songs were composed by the Triumvirate's leading maestro. Many began to bustle about the Royal Theatre in hopes of catching a glimpse of rehearsals or hearing an early piece of music, but the surprise would be well-kept if only to excite interest, and the spectators must therefore wait until the projected opening night.

While the chief of Frewyn's denizens were left to imagine all the wondrous machinations taking place within the auspices of the theatre walls, two of the keep's residents were treated to an accidental and early prospect of the goings-on. Although many of the kingdom's nobility milled about the parapets of Diras Castle, determined to see the rehearsals by leaning over the merlons of the western battlements, Teague and Mureadh were the first two to discern the character of the new play. They were engaged to spend the evening with Connors and Nerri, and after a long day of training in the keep's yard and running his majesty's errands, they had cleansed themselves in the barracks and were on their way back to the soldier's mess from using the facilities when an argument taking place outside the theatre entrance caught their attention. They stopped once quitting the latrine tower, hid behind an adjacent wall to screen themselves from view, and overheard the director of the piece according someone a most stern reproof.

The remonstrance was understood well enough: something about the new poster was incorrect, someone's name was not quite as large as it should have been, someone else's name was far too eclipsing, the colours were too strong, the style too fanciful, the printing too plain, and upon the whole, the announcement must be entirely remade. This was of course refuted by its illustrator, but even the carefully-chosen paints and detailed illustration of the principle characters would not do; the size of the names must reflect the director's brilliance, the art must portray a realistic genius, and nothing less would be tolerated.

When the argument had done, the assertions heated on the director's side and the refutations muted on the artist's, the director returned to the theatre to officiate the remainder of the day's practice and the illustrator was left to sulk and grumble. He remarked his work, and after a moment's consideration, humphed and placed the poster onto the billboard. Bitterness and anger were what drove his actions, but the satisfaction in seeing his glorious work displayed on the billboard of the Royal Theatre even for a few minutes together before someone should come and take it down was all his triumph. He stood back from it after having secured it in place, folded his arms across his chest, and spied the poster with a complacent grin. The names were too small to be sure, but the images of the three main characters were the centerpiece and glory of the work.

A moment passed and the illustrator was suddenly called into the theatre. One of the sets must be repainted, and without a thought, he hastened inside, leaving the poster on the billboard for Teague and Mureadh to investigate. They crawled out from their position behind the wall of the latrine tower and before they had taken a few steps were struck with the sudden shock of what the advertisement depicted: a fair-haired and large-breasted woman dressed in little more than a few garnishings was being held by an enormous and fur-clad beast, one with terrible fangs, unforgiveable underbite, and glowing red eyes; behind the gruesome ogre and his swooning damsel was a handsome king, riding a bucking horse and waving a golden broadsword in the air. What the image had meant to suggest was clear enough by the commander's distinguishable attributes, by the Den Asaan's ferocious features, and by the king's handsome aspect, but the title across the top of the piece secured all their worries. If the heading of the play was not enough to convince them of this opera being a farce, the tagline of "Two hearts, two warring nations, one forbidden love" written across the bottom certainly was. The names of the directors, writers and everyone involved were unimportant where the subject of the play was concerned, and Mureadh cringed in aversion to think of what their superior officers and the king would say while Teague only sighed and shook his head.

When the first wave of horror had done with them, Teague and Mureadh stepped closer to examine the poster, Teague carefully collecting the names of every person responsible for this nonsense — that he might relay them to the Den Asaan when they should no doubt be demanded — and Mureadh unable to do anything other than gawp in dread.

"Well," Teague said, after a few moments of silence, "It is painted very well, even if the colours are incorrect. He's obviously a gifted artist. It's a shame that his talent was used for this."

Mureadh was far too horrified to reply: his superior officer, one well-known for his intolerance of inanity, was being mocked, and his mate, over whom the giant was particularly possessive, was being debased. Such an image was certain to offend and incite the Den Asaan, and Mureadh scrambled to remove it from the billboard before anyone else should see it and laugh at its subject.

The announcement did not distress Teague as much as it did Mureadh; he knew that the commander would have an excellent laugh over the artwork, but he could not feel the same where King Alasdair and the Den Asaan were concerned. Were the opera to depict the events of the war in a truthful manner, he should have no scruple in allowing the production to continue as planned, but as the Den Asaan was here shown as a snarling and hideous creature with glowing eyes and woeful countenance, he could have no doubt of the opera's pretense. Teague made a heavy sigh and took the folded poster from Mureadh's hands. "I'll tell the commander," he said, walking back toward the barracks.

"Should I tell the Den Asaan?" said Mureadh, almost terrified of the reaction such a revelation must produce.

Teague stopped and considered how they had best proceed. "No," he decided presently. "I think we should let her tell the Den Asaan. She knows how to calm him." He looked down at the folded poster in his hand and added, "Well, she knows how to keep him from killing those who disparage her." He smirked, tucked the poster under his arm, and turned back toward the castle, rubbing his hands together with secret joy, hardly able to wait and see what sort of uproar this kind of travesty should construct.

# CHAPTER THREE
## PARDON

he early evening sky was beginning to favour the capital with its vibrant hues, and the commander remarked the coming of night from her place in the barracks while discussing with Tomas where the new weapon racks were to be placed along the far wall of the yard. She heard a few of the blacksmith's quiet and humble words, but the brilliancy of the setting sun made her not much able to attend.

"I'll put the light weapons in the corners and keep the wall space for the swords," was Tomas' smiling conclusion once he realized the commander was gazing out the window and looking wistfully at the sky. He observed the amber light ebbing out from behind the few clouds and felt all the sanguine reverie the commander exuded. "Makes me feel like I'm home again, aye," he said in a soft voice, thinking of the small house he and his mother had kept in Westren.

The commander hummed in agreement and continued to inspect the various linings of the clouds. "There is something about the prospect of a gloaming sky that reminds one of Frewyn's more verdant downs," she said, at last turning to the blacksmith. "It is a shame, however, that Frewyn sunsets are so early in the autumn months and can therefore never be properly appreciated when one is busy training young lords to be useful or being bade to cook for a giant of certain distinction."

Tomas laughed his diffident chuff, bowed his parting, and turned toward the entrance to the yeoman's quarter only to discover Teague standing in the archway with a concerned look on his face. He said his quiet hellos, made a polite bow, and caught a glimpse of the image on a certain folded poster being taken from under his arm. Tomas shuddered and rubbed his brow as he passed out of the garrison. "I'm goin' te have te make a whole new row of trainin' dummies when this is over," he murmured to himself, and returned to his smith to tell Shayne of the destruction awaiting the implements in the yard which both of them had just recently erected.

Teague made a chary approach, wondering how to broach the subject in a manner that would not give offense. He said his addresses to the commander, explained what he and Mureadh had seen, and before he could finish his speech with a solemn regret and apology for the affront on behalf of the Frewyn Players, the commander interposed with:

"I must have evidence of this travesty," she said, beaming with glee. "This is far too much suspense."

He produced the poster and smiled at the commander's instant eagerness as she took it into her hands and held it open for a meticulous inspection.

"Oh, by the Gods, this is glorious," she exclaimed, remarking the whole of the piece. "I must show this to my mate. I cannot decide what shall anger him most: the violet skin, the overdrawn and yet handsome scowl, the fangs, or the paltry sizes of his sword, kilt, and the article beneath it." She smirked at such an erroneous interpretation and nodded while her eye perused every corner of the page. "This depiction could only be made more marvelous if a rose had been put in his mouth," she said laughingly. She sighed and her expression saddened. "He shall be disappointed about the size of my chest, however."

"I did think that was a little inaccurate," said Teague, stealing a momentary glance at the deep vale between the commander's heavy breasts.

"Little is certainly what I should call those in comparison to what my mate so delights in every evening."

They exchanged a smile, and the commander shifted into the light to remark the vibrancy of the colours and the brushstrokes employed in the piece.

"The palette was well chosen," she mused. "I rather like my flaxen hair and blue eyes."

"The Den Asaan's pink kilt is my particular favourite," Teague said with a half-smile.

"Pink is rather his colour, especially with the red eyes and grey hair to match. He's made me far too becoming and much too small in height and in proportion. I'm rather inclined to think this charade is not even about me, as I am nowhere on this advertisement other than in the title, and even that is ambiguous. My mate is certainly recognizable."

Teague simpered. "I recognized him immediately."

"I assume that this pristine fellow on the glimmering horse is meant to be our good king."

"I believe so, commander. "

"Well, Alasdair looks rather splendid, as he ought. He shall be quite pleased. Any illustration that portrays Alasdair with such excellently sculpted hair and a fine jerkin is all his delight. Maeve is the one who should be offended. She should never have wanted to be a white horse nor this fat and smiling."

Teague chuckled to himself, relieved to see how keen the commander was to oblige such misconception, and as she excused herself and hastened to the kitchen to share the news with Alasdair, he hoped that the offense on the king's side would be as moderate as the commander's. Though he did wish to remain within Diras Castle to see Rautu's reaction to the advertisement, there was a dinner to be had and there were friends to be met with, and as he left the barracks to rejoin Mureadh, he had little doubt of hearing the giant's roaring disapproval from wherever he should be in the capital at the moment of discovery.

Upon reaching the keep's kitchen, the commander found Alasdair sitting at the table with his early evening tea, reading over his proclamations for the day. He seemed equanimity itself now that his presiding in the royal courts for the day had done: leaning back in his favourite chair, with half a glance toward the yard and half toward his papers, his hand in mid-ascension, the teacup pressed against his lips, expecting to be soothed by his first sip of lemon soother, when the advertisement was thrust before him, causing him to replace his cup upon the table and investigate the announcement directly.

"Oh, this looks brilliant," Alasdair declared smilingly. "Is this about us?"

"I daresay it is," the commander said, pointing to the title of the opera, "although I'm hardly recognizable."

"Well, I can tell it's you by the . . ." Alasdair made a suggestive gesture toward her chest and left his assertion there, returning his gaze to the poster while a small blush crept up his cheek.

"Those are far too small to be mine."

The size and shape of her magnanimous proportions could be compared, but Alasdair would not look again; he would not be suspected of gawping for pleasure nor would his gentlemanly sensibilities allow him to be baited so easily. "I suppose you're right," he said quickly, keeping his gaze firmly upon the advertisement. He seemed bemused, and pointing to the heroic figure in the piece said, "Is that meant to be me on that white horse?"

"And I do believe that's meant to be Maeve."

Alasdair raised a brow. "She would be disappointed."

"As she should be. What chestnut mare wants to be a white stallion?"

"And she certainly isn't that . . ." fat was what he wished to say, but at that moment, Martje had trundled in from the larder and Alasdair was forced to check himself. He said a polite hello and his features flushed with colour to think he had almost said the forbidden word in the plump cook's presence. "I look very well, though," he said cheerfully. "My hair is tidy and my jerkin looks very fitting. Those breeches, though, don't go well with those boots. It would have been better to match them with calfskin boots, not these impossible things. Who would wear boots that low when riding? The fabric would chafe, surely."

The commander laughed and shook her head. "Is that all your worry?"

"Yes, I think so," he said with stout confidence. He took a moment to regard the remainder of the piece and then decided, "Well, Rautu looks accurate, doesn't he."

"You are too horrid," she said with a sagacious smile.

"I'm allowed to say what I want when he's not here."

"You know that he has eyes and ears in every corner of this keep and yet you would ridicule him. You are all bravery, Alasdair."

"If he can say whatever he wants to my face, then I think I might be allowed to admire his portrait before demands to kill the illustrator." Alasdair made a defensive humph and began folding the poster. "Has he seen it yet?"

"No."

"Good. I'll send the herald to the theatre with the instruction that everyone involved with this production is to leave the capital immediately."

"You are the epitome of charity, Alasdair, in giving them such a warning, but I daresay he shall hunt them down and skin them regardless. Will you allow this opera to be performed even though you know its content to be possibly disparaging?"

Alasdair made an abashed smile and took a last peek at the depiction of himself. "I wonder if they'll have me kill Rautu in a terrific duel or if I'll merely sing him to death."

"You know the powers of the Frewyn Players and their ability to depict historical events with perfect accuracy."

It was said with such wryness that Alasdair was forced to agree with her; the portrayal of Mad Queen Maeve, though highly entertaining, could hardly be supposed a truthful display when all of Frewyn was aware that her end came from her insanity and not from the edge of an envious lover's knife as the play might have the uninformed believe. They laughed and sighed, both of them in equal dread and anticipation of what such a piece could depict, and stood from the kitchen table, the commander desirous of telling her mate before he could find out from another quarter and Alasdair wanting to visit the tailor.

"If they portray my mate as a snarling and murderous beast, he shall make their interpretation an actuality," the commander warned as they began walking toward the main hall.

"It could be me who gets trounced on stage."

"That is rather impossible, Alasdair. My mate kills his opponents, and as this boasts of being an accurate depiction," she said, gesturing toward the poster in Alasdair's hand, "you cannot have been defeated, for you are standing in front of me."

"That is true, but I'm certain Carrigh wouldn't mind seeing me beaten by a giant after I've ruined these breeches she just fixed for me."

Alasdair looked sorrowfully at his knee where a single thread was out of place along the inner seam. He groaned to himself, cursing the chairs in the royal courts for being unkind to such delicate fabric and fine stitching, but was soon consoled when thinking of being bare before his wife in the privacy of the tailor while watching her mend his garments, her loveliness expatiated by the glow of light pervading the tailor window. He could watch her at her sewing table for hours, her features intent on her work, her delicate and nimble hands creating every stitch. His sighs of mild anxiety became wistful exhalations, and soon he was only too eager to visit the tailor and show Carrigh how heroically he had been portrayed. He said his good evenings to the commander and hastened away to the servants' quarter, passing the Cuineills' apartments and entering the tailor, where he found his wife, sitting at her sewing table and appearing as beautiful as ever: the warmth of her skin summoned by the amber light from beyond the window, her golden curls illuminated by the tender glow from the lit candle beside her, her upright and slender form in perfect posture finely shaped by the outline of her simple dress. His breath was nearly lost at such a prospect: a stunning creature hidden away for his personal reflection and delight. He closed the door behind him as she turned to greet her husband and king, and he reckoned that though he might never truly win in a duel against the Den Asaan, his prize came to him in the doting wife who was quickly approaching him, kissing his cheek, and regarding him with the most devoted looks he had ever been accorded. The governance she had over his heart was unmistakable; a kiss from her granted another from him, one more eager and more passionate than she was prepared to receive. He cradled her in his arms and consumed her, enjoying the tenderness of her lips, the warmth of her touch, and the mellifluous fragrance of her sinuous skin.

Alasdair released her and said in a low voice, "I apologize, my darling, but I've brought something for you to fix."

Carrigh looked down and half-smiled. "Do you mean the torn seam in your breeches or what you have beneath them, sire?"

Alasdair turned his face to the side, moderately and happily ashamed. "It can be both, if you aren't too upset with me for ruining your hard work."

"I think I can forgive you, sire," she whispered, pressing herself against him and untying the front of his breeches.

Alasdair tossed the poster onto the sewing table and asked whether his wife would forgive him standing or leaning over. She preferred that exoneration be granted in various places about the tailor, and before Alasdair was able to remove his breeches entirely, he was already receiving his forgiveness by way of a kneeling seamstress, of her dexterous hands and an eager mouth. Alasdair froze in place, rapt by the pleasance her fervor afforded him. Soon, however, he could no longer bear her means of forgiveness and must give way to his desires of providing her with his due apologies. He lifted her from the ground and brought her to the sewing table where he might beg to be forgiven and she might cry out her breathless pardon with each penetration her husband should supply.

A lifting of her skirts, a maneuvering of her garments, and he was prepared to ask while she was more than prepared to receive his contrition. A few moments were spent glorying in his wife's long and lean legs, her lithe flesh, and her small round backside, and when he could wait no longer, he leaned over his wife, lifted her leg against the sewing table, and enjoyed his ardent repentance. His thrusts were measured while her crevice was yet unaccustomed to his size, but the more she accepted him, the faster his penetrations became. He osculated her arched back between his aggressive drives and he reveled in hearing her muffled cries of clemency. He gripped her hips and forced his extent within her. Her cries grew strident and her words of pardon soon became entreaties for penitence. Alasdair indulged her, driving unreservedly into her until he felt her contract around him. She writhed beneath him, her fingers gripping the edge of the table, moaning through her arrival, compelling him to meet her completion. He did presently, and enjoyed her gentle ripples matching the rhythm of his own.

He leaned down once he had done, kissed his wife's cheek, and said, "Do you forgive me?" in a tender tone.

Carrigh giggled to herself. She could never have supposed herself angry with him for something that was so easily fixed and was inclined to say no if only to incur another bout of his contrition. "I forgive you, sire," she said, smiling.

They exchanged a most devoted kiss. Carrigh returned to her seat at the table and bade Alasdair to remove his breeches from around his feet. She began mending them whilst making intermittent glances at the king beside her, glorying in his smiles and admiring the advertisement he began showing her. She could look, but could not much attend, for the King of Frewyn was standing in her tailor, half-dressed and his complexion in a glow of affection for the pleasurable pardon he had just been awarded.

# CHAPTER FOUR
## "YOU ARE CORDIALLY INVITED"

Within a few minutes, the mending work was done, and while Alasdair was at liberty to redress, Carrigh was given the poster for her assessment of how well her king looked. She laughed at its absurdity, declaring that her husband was far more becoming in person than he was in the illustration, for a self-important royal on a white stead would never do for her where a humble king on a chestnut mare had exceeded all of her expectations.

"Does the subject of the opera bother you?" said Alasdair in a caring voice, taking Carrigh's hand and pressing it to his heart.

"Not at all, sire. It does seem to be a romantic play, but don't all Marridon operas end in tragedy? This play might offend you ever much more so than it could me, sire. They might show you losing a duel to the Den Asaan."

"I could win against him if I wanted to," Alasdair pouted. "I simply choose to fight my battles in a court rather than on a field."

The defensive conviction must be allowed where Alasdair's feelings were mentioned, and Carrigh only smiled at her husband's declaration, permitting him to believe as he liked. Her attention, however, was soon drawn to the glimmering jerkin that Alasdair's flamboyant counterpart was wearing in the piece. "Would you really wear something with that much trimming?" was Carrigh's simpering question.

Alasdair looked almost ashamed. "Well," said he, turning aside, "I was going to ask if you could make something similar.

I'd like to wear it for the opening night." He observed her surprised countenance and hastily amended, "To keep with the accuracy of the play, of course."

"Of course, sire." She giggled and shook her head. She should have taken it as a matter of course that her king would wish to look the part. She postulated, searched about her for the requisite materials, and then said, "I think I have what I need to make something similar. I can have it finished by the end of the evening, but I refuse to put golden tassels on your shoulders."

Alasdair feigned a groan of discontent and then smiled and thanked his wife for indulging his fancies. He knew it was an unreasonable contrivance, wanting to be the image of so gallant a depiction, but it would only be for one evening and then he may be reasonable again. He left Carrigh to her work and went to find the herald to make his proper warnings to the Frewyn Players, but when he walked toward the herald's office in quest of his messenger, he discovered him just leaving with a stack of what appeared to be invitations in his hands.

"Majesty," the herald said, rushing toward him. "This is for you." He forced one of the invitations into the king's hands, bowed and hastened away before his king could hinder him from his most important task.

"Wait," Alasdair called after him, but he was already gone, and any warning that he could give him with regard to the opera must be relinquished. He looked down at the summons in his hand, read its brief message, and sighed in renewed vexation. "This isn't going to end well," he said to himself. He considered having the play disbanded, but his curiosity to see how the production would end overruled his judgment and the opera would go on.

The herald leapt through the whole of the keep, leaving one invitation at the foot of every door in each quarter of the castle. Many thanked him and gave their assenting replies with all due expediency, and though he required only a yes or no with regard to the given addressees' attendance, there was one attendant's reply which the herald did not think it worth waiting to receive. Once he had delivered every other invitation, he made his way to the commons. He mounted the winding stair at the end of the main hall and stopped at the foot of the threshold to stare at the door with a horrified expression. He was sensible of the reply he would receive from the commons' inhabitants. He considered the pain he might suffer from delivering the invitation here and contrived to set it down and flee as quickly as his legs would allow. He calmed his rapidly beating heart, told himself that the beast usually lurking within was out hunting at this hour, and flung the invitation at the door as soon as he had the courage for it. With the delivery made, he turned to descend the stair, all pride and complacence for having delivered the message without an altercation, but the moment he took the first step toward the stairs, he found himself suddenly on the ground. He lay beneath the archway for some minutes before venturing to open his eyes. It felt as though he had bumped into something, though he had seen nothing but the winding steps, but in opening his eyes and staring at the Den Asaan's large and bare feet, he recollected a slight flash of movement from the ceiling of the stair before his landing on the floor.

"Why are you at my door, messenger?" a sonorous voice from above rumbled.

Fear overpowered the herald, and he kept his eyes low in hopes of being spared the Den Asaan's pointing finger and flouting countenance. "I came to deliver an invitation to you, Den Asaan," he stammered.

Rautu growled and stepped over the herald's shivering form to where the summons had landed. He peered down at the direction of the invitation: it was addressed to his mate and himself, had come from the Royal Theatre — certainly not the most abominable place in the world — but the sight most infuriating to him was a small image drawn beside the address of a scowling monster holding a small and swooning woman in one hand while balancing a rose in his mouth. He had little idea who the woman was until he deciphered himself by the molded hair and familiar trappings. His eyes narrowed, his lips tensed, and any anger that such a mockery could excite was beginning to surface. "Leave my home," he demanded.

The herald stood, thanked the giant for his mercy, and fled down the winding stair, praising the Gods that his life had been spared and praying that the Frewyn Players should share in his good fortune.

Rautu waited until the herald had gone to take the invitation into his hand. He smelled its thick paper, licked its corners to test for poison, and inspected the meticulous handwriting for any other secret meaning contained in the finely made letters. Once he declared the message safe, he turned it over and read thus:

*You are cordially invited to attend the first ever Frewyn Players' production of "The Commander and the Den Asaan Rautu: An opera in three acts", to begin tomorrow evening at sundown, with playbook by Frewyn's Sealin MacBryde and with songs and direction by Marridon's own Baronus Tilney.*

The invitation went on to list the principle actors and supporting cast, but the phrase *you are cordially invited* followed by the two names of those most responsible for this censure was all the shamelessness the Den Asaan could endure. Such a slight towards himself was easily recovered from: a challenge might be used to both of the culpable parties and therefore his pride could salvaged, but the insult he felt on his mate's side, the dishonour of her being portrayed as a weak and swooning damsel, and the further disrepute of being so affably invited to witness it, was an unfathomable wrong. His arms shook at his sides, his fist clenched around the invitation, and he felt his rage overtake him. He would have his revenge for this gratuitous ridicule, he would destroy everyone responsible for such unmitigated debasement, but before he could descend the stair and make his way toward the Royal Theatre, he was stopped by his mate, who upon hearing the bustle outside of the commons, opened the door to the main room where she had been sitting, and drew his attention by saying, "Did you destroy the invitation before or after you read it?"

Rautu turned to see the commander standing in the doorway of the commons with an invitation of her own in her hand. "How did you obtain that?" he said, calming slightly.

"The herald, though decent in his duties due to your constant coddling, is not perfect, as you well know."

"Hmph."

"He had dropped this on his way to the kitchen to give your friend Martje her invitation to this nonsense." She paused and smirked at her mate. "You realize we must go if only to jeer."

"Your king allowed this?" Rautu growled, stabbing his finger toward the invitation.

"I don't think he would have had he known about it. Teague and Mureadh made the discovery." She remarked the illustration on the invitation and shrugged. "I do wonder if they'll have me hopping about on stage in scanty furs or merely have me topless to keep the eyes of their audience from glazing over." She simpered and looked up to find Rautu unable and unwilling to share her mirth. "Do you mean to skin everyone responsible for this farce or just the director?"

"Everyone."

"Well, you certainly mean to be thorough."

Rautu plucked the invitation from her hand, and with a firm glower said, "You will not attend this performance, Traala."

"And why should I not go? I cannot miss you recanting your woes through warbling song. And besides, I want to see the gorgeous and melancholic woman they chose to play my role."

"Your people will see that and believe it is an accurate representation of you."

"Iimon Ghaala," she said sweetly, tugging the ends of his locks. "It's meant to be a parody, or at least it shall be to the Frewyns who see it. Everyone knows what truly happened well enough, I think."

"My people would not do this," Rautu asserted, his tranquility returning with each pleasing and circular motion his mate's fingers made. "Our songs and dances honour our legends and our champions. We do not deride those responsible for our wellbeing." He looked away and said in a quiet voice, "I will not allow them to mock you, Traala."

The commander gave the giant a tender smile. "Such devotion," she cooed, her eyes sparkling. "I daresay you would burn down the whole theatre if only to defend my honour."

"I would." He observed her with a reverent fondness and pulled her into the bend of his arm. "You will not go until I have seen this performance," he purred in her ear. "I will judge whether it is acceptable for others to watch."

"So you shall see Alasdair's counterpart frolic about on a horse made from a broom? Hardly fair that I should miss it."

Her remonstrances were silenced by a kiss from the giant, and without another word, he took his sword into his hand, leapt down the winding stair, and thundered toward the Royal Theatre, prepared to acquit or reprove as the situation would warrant.

# Chapter Five
# The Director

The evening hum of voices in the keep began to increase. Whispers of where the giant was going and who had merited his wrath excited the general intrigue about the castle. Heads leaned out of open windows, eyes peered over sills, spectators watched from the peristyle, and by the time the giant had reached the double doors of the Royal Theatre, every inhabitant of the Diras castle keep was watching his movements. Here was a feast of entertainment, for what amusement could an opera provide when a giant clad in furs and holding an immense black blade was pounding his fist against the theatre door and roaring for attention. The nobles and yeoman in the peristyle cooed with delight, and some even pretended to be besieged by the sudden desire to visit the latrine tower if only to have the prime view of Rautu's retaliation. Those who were brave enough to stand near the giant cowered when hearing his strident demands.

"I will speak to the creator of this performance," he bellowed. He waited a few moments for a reply but none came. With his first and decidedly civil request ignored, his patience with this affair was finally spent. His anger frothed, his mind seethed, and he prepared to slice off the hook lock from the door when a small slit in one of the entrance's crevices suddenly moved to reveal a pair of wide eyes staring at him in horror.

Trembling on the other side of the door was the director's assistant. He had been sent to kindly convey that the company would only be admitting herald and similar press agents during rehearsals, but when he had heard the violent wrawl of their production's true counterpart, all of the assistant's audacity and self-governance had gone. He debated for some minutes whether to open the door or merely not to respond at all, but he feared that to keep Frewyn's tempestuous beast waiting would only bring more mischief. He had therefore opened the slot, and when he saw the giant's livid expression had instantly thought to close it again when the giant wedged his fingers against the latch to keep it open. He yelped and shook with fright, hardly knowing what to say that would not anger the beast further. "Oh, Den Asaan!" the assistant said, laughing timorously. "How honoured we are to have you here."

"If you were honoured, you would open this door and greet me with respect," Rautu growled.

The assistant felt any small measure of courage he may have yet had begin to fail him. He desperately wished to run away, but to leave the door would secure the giant's following. "I'm sorry, Den Asaan," he said in a dreadful hush, "but I am forbidden from opening this door to anyone who is not here to advertise the play."

Rautu's lips pursed and his hand tightened around his blade. "Bring me your superior. I will speak with him."

The assistant was acquitted his deleterious duties, and he said his praises to the Gods as he leapt away to retrieve the director. He hastened to the stage where the Players were in the midst of rehearsing the third act, and the moment he called out that the Den Asaan was at the front door demanding to speak with the director of the piece, the actors gave one another apprehensive looks and went to hide behind the sets along with the illustrator, who had just finished repainting a few of the sets and was now wishing he had not left the poster upon the billboard. There was only one among them who was overjoyed at the Den Asaan's arrival: the director, Baronus Tilney, leapt up from his seat in the front row of the theatre, clapped his hands together in glee, and hurried off to greet the giant. The Frewyn Players and the entire orchestra watched their director hasten up the aisle and not one of them held a shred of hope for his safe return.

Baronus Tilney was a flamboyant man: his suit was decorated in the traditional Marridon style, tight and tailored, adorned with watch fobs and ornamented with thin gold chains draping from every little pocket; his hair was swept to one side, his moustache was voluminous and curled; and though he was gangly and made fluid gestures when he spoke, his air was so unprepossessing as to make him excessively unpleasing. He was used to being the most celebrated director in all of Marridon, and though he was no one in Frewyn, the kingdom that could not appreciate opera or any style of high class entertainment in his estimation, he walked about with a complacent countenance and would have his own way in everything. He had never met the commander or the Den Asaan, but felt he knew enough about them from the account Marridon's chief reporter had given: the woman was an unkempt and clever farmer who happened to be able to fight and command an army by the power of her chest, and the giant was a ferocious ogre who was only calmed when eating chocolate, swinging his sword, and lying atop his woman. He had felt that these were precise descriptions of Frewyn's uncivilized heroes until he came to the door and through the unopened slot beheld how immense and petrifying the beast truly was. He perceived the furs, the scowl, the judging glare, everything to mark the creature as hostile, but instead of shrinking from the fierce creature, he opened the door and made an ostentatious bow. "Ah, the honourable Den Asaan!" he cried, making a flourish. "How pleased I am that you heard of our little production." He curled the ends of his moustache and spied the giant with a triumphant smile.

Rautu, somewhat confused by the director's exultation, stood back when Tilney opened his arms as though he meant to embrace him. "You will not touch me, Dhargovhari," he demanded, holding his sword toward the director.

Tilney laughed affectedly. "My, you are just as unsociable as I have heard! I think you'll find our recreation of you quite correct, but I'm sorry to say, honoured Den Asaan, that the performance doesn't begin until tomorrow evening. It is the greatest compliment in the world to me that you should be so eager to see our little show, but as of now we are in the middle of rehearsals and I cannot let you inside."

The brashness of supposing a depiction of himself as accurate was ill-judgment enough, but the self-satisfaction with which it was said and the barring of the Den Asaan from the Royal Theatre was an affront too great to tolerate. The director's smiling assertions and elegant snideness only heightened his faults, and where others might have permitted such a humour for a director of his apparent distinction, the Den Asaan would make no such allowances. In one swift motion, he grabbed the ends of Tilney's moustache, twisted them together, and held them up, forcing the director to stand on his toes and make a wincing smile. "You will hear me," Rautu's voice rumbled.

"I'm listening to you, sir," Tilney whimpered, endeavoring to keep his moustache from tearing by dancing about on the tips of his feet.

"You will allow me to see this performance before you show it to the rest of Frewyn. You have chosen to tell the story of me and my mate. She is my chosen Ataas Traala. Therefore, I will make certain that your representation is accurate."

The director was then released, and after he recurled his moustache and adjusted his fitted suit, he said, "If you will give me a few moments, honourable Den Asaan, I will notify the actors and we can have a dress rehearsal for you." It was said with condescension, more toward the giant's supposed inability to appreciate his work and the time requisite to create such a masterpiece of the stage, and less toward the giant's powers of understanding. He cleared his throat, turned up his nose, retied his cravat and said, "It will not be perfect, but since you insist. Please do be good enough to wait here." He turned directly and reentered the theatre with a sharp huff and a stamping of his feet.

While others may have harboured considerations of flight for the renewed anger the Den Asaan conveyed, the director took the Den Asaan's orders as a challenge. He marched back to the stage, called out for his actors to attend him, and told them that they were to quickly run through the ending of the play, the director determined to impress with his craft and the company certain to be unequal to such high expectations. They insisted upon changing the names of the principle characters at least, making them some other commander and some other giant, changing the name of the kingdom — or perhaps it would not be a kingdom at all — and changing the king for a knight from Gallei, but no suggestion would do; it must be the Den Asaan, it must be the woman commander, it must be the King of Frewyn, and where the Frewyn Players were once elated to be exhibiting a new piece, they would have gladly traded in every new set and costume to be performing Mad Queen Maeve again. The director's pride and vanity won, and "The Commander and the Den Asaan Rautu: the Opera" would go on.

# CHAPTER SIX
## RETRIBUTION

For twenty minutes did the Den Asaan sit at the door to the theatre, his sword in his hand and his mind rapt in rumination. Those who observed him wondered at whether he were preparing for a duel or if he were saying the Haanta Haakhas in honour of those he was on the precipice of decimating. Some of the spectators watching from the peristyle were unaware of the giant's tranquilizing ritual, but Teague, Mureadh, Nerri and Connors were more than sensible of their commander's custom. They had just returned from their evening in the capital, and after delighting in an excellent meal at the Wayward Traveler were disposed to return to the keep for a game of Jainsago in the soldier's mess whereupon entering the castle through the yeoman's quarter they descried the Den Asaan sitting in his meditative state. They stopped, gave one another misgiving looks, and began to wonder how long it should be before the giant's forbearance with Marridon's premiere genius would perish. They watched and waited, fidgeted, raised brows, and when the Den Asaan did not move, they stared at one another in happy amazement.

"When you said there was an adaptation of how the two commanders met being put on," said Connors to Teague and Mureadh, "I believed you. But what I didn't believe is how well he would take it."

"This *is* calm for him," observed Nerri, frowning in surprise.

Teague made a roguish grin. "Perhaps their acting abilities aren't so terrible after all."

"What do you mean?" asked Mureadh.

"Someone had to pacify him, and the commander is not around."

"How many people do you think it took to appease him?" asked Connors smilingly.

"If he's sitting there and waiting, probably only one. A crowd would have incited him." Teague laughed to himself and imagined the Frewyn Players scrambling about, some of them cultivating enough chocolate to quiet the giant and others contriving to hide those responsible for the charade. He simpered and shook his head, and beginning to walk toward the main hall said, "He enjoys giving his prey a chance to prove themselves before taking them to the hunting grounds. I only hope that the play is as good as the excuse they gave him to keep him outside, because if it isn't, he is going to be even angrier than he was before."

"Should we notify the commander?" asked Mureadh as he passed with the others into the hallway.

Teague looked back, the corners of his mouth curling slightly. "I'm certain she already knows," he said, and though the chief of his interest still lay in the Den Asaan and the fate of the Frewyn Players, there were pockets to empty and mulled wine to be had, and all his concern soon became how well he would play at his favourite game.

Mureadh, however, could not be so easy. He worried more for the Den Asaan than he did for the Players, for he believed that whatever insult they wished to rely to his commanding officer was worth all the violent retribution it could produce. His only scruple was in having the whole of the keep watch the giant release his ethnaa as though it were nothing but a mere amusement. He understood the giant's unbearable affliction and knew its agonies, but where he was sensible of this, many others were not. He felt Rautu justified in any retribution he should see fit to exact and did not wish to have his superior ridiculed and degraded only for doing what he would have done himself.

Connors as well felt obliged to agonize, and though his concerns were trifling in comparison to Mureadh's, he could not be rid of them with any tolerable alacrity. He must be the great worrier of the four, and where propriety and duty to the king were concerned, his vexation must follow. He wondered at how Alasdair could allow this to endure, if not for his own reputation than for the queen's. Carrigh was an understanding and amiable woman, but would not the play offend her to show her husband pining over one for whom he had only ever retained a shadow of interest? He felt for her exceedingly, and was on the point of conveying his concerns to the king when the new pack of cards was broken open, coppers were tossed onto the table, and his losses at Jainsago were impending. He must leave the majesties' fate to themselves, but he would be the first one to answer the king and queen's summons should there be one, his heeding them made ever more celeritous by the lightness of newly emptied pockets.

News of the perching giant soon spread throughout the keep. Fifteen minutes spent in high expectancy brought with it all the due attention, and once the report had reached Alasdair, he called the commander down to the kitchen. His object was to discuss if they had better not request a few alterations to the play, but when he spoke his apprehensions, Martje ardently refuted such a retraction. She and Shayne had been sitting at the table enjoying a small supper together when the herald had come to give them their invitation, and the instant Martje beheld the image on the card, there was the end to all peace in the business. She laughed and hollered and slapped her knees, her eyes watered with revelrous mirth, and she declared the depiction the most exceptional likeness she had ever seen.

"You had better hold onto it, Martje," the commander said with half a smile. "If my mate doesn't approve their performance, that invitation shall be your only remembrance of the opera that never was."

"Sure, I'm not missin' this," Martje asserted with great animation, stabbing a finger at the invitation in her opposing hand. "Shayne is gonna frame this here drawin' so I can hang it in the larder. I'm gonna ask the Larkins to make a bust out of it, one with a nice space in the mouth so I can change the rose every day. Maybe I'll ask him to make it a bird bath, one of those with a little fountain and all."

"I should very much like to see this article when it is made. The only manner in which my mate shall not destroy it is if you promise to make the fountain a chocolate one."

"Naw, kin. Then the beast'll be near it all day," Martje scoffed. "I want it for myself so's I can admire it and watch the birds enjoyin' themselves. Maybe I'll have Shayne put it by the cottage."

Shayne looked as though he had little idea of installing anything so obtrusive and odd near their small home in Tyferrim and grumbled something about having another thing about the house to fix.

Although he did not wish to ruin Martje's jovial musings, Alasdair felt he must interpose here. "I'm sorry, Martje, but even though we all want to see this production, I think it best to—"

"You can't do this to me, Majesty," Martje begged, holding her hands together in supplication, her eyes wide with the horror of losing her most precious reprisal. "I've been gaggin' for a chance to see that monster get what's comin' to him. Please let it go on for one night and please let me see it. He's been eatin' us out of house and home since he came here. A poor cook can't have revenge any other way."

"You did try to poison him once," the commander murmured.

Martje gave the commander a sharp look. "You never told me he could eat the stuff without so much as a blink!"

"I didn't think there was a need to tell you. I am still astonished as to how you tricked him into eating those potatoes knowing that they were made by your hands. Perhaps he knew they were poisoned and ate them to spite you."

"Never you mind, kin," Martje huffed. "I wanna see this here play, and that's that." She pouted, stomped her foot, and folded her arms, and would not allow another word to be said that was not one of approbation for the play's continuance.

The commander smiled at Alasdair. "I think we must allow for some retribution on Martje's behalf, don't you?"

"Well," Alasdair began his relent, but he need not finish; Martje was already praising him to the Gods and leaping up and down in exultation.

"Why don't we all attend this rehearsal?" was the commander's suggestion, said with eyes twinkling in arch interest. "It certainly concerns us, and with the fervent demand of the Frewyn King, I daresay we shall all be granted admittance."

To have Carrigh see him in so triumphant a pose might be worth the venture. She had already assured him that the play's subject had not offended her, and therefore if it could now only endear and delight. Alasdair agreed that they should all go, go now and go together, and the instant his decree was pronounced, the commander went to the soldier's mess to gather those playing cards in exchange for a more exciting diversion, Martje threw off her apron and demanded that she and Shayne assemble the Cuineills, and Alasdair went to the tailor to find his wife just having tied off the last stitch in the jerkin he was to wear to the theatre.

# CHAPTER SEVEN
# THE OPERA

The jerkin was donned, the Cuineills were got, the mantles and redingotes were fastened, and everyone was soon arrived at the Royal Theatre. The commander, however, broke from the party for a few moments on account of a most necessary call to Diras Delights. The Frewyn bakery was just closing for the day and therefore had little to recommend its usual excellent stock, but she declared herself prepared to take away anything that was tolerably fresh and not the least bit wholesome. She was given a few of the chocolate toffee butter biscuits for her visit, and though she was warned that they were from yesterday, they must do for now. If a play was to be sat out, it would not be sat out in penance, for an opera was the most excruciating sort of entertainment in the world and could only be borne by eating more insalubrious yet delicious items than is good for one. The procurance was chiefly made for the Den Asaan, whose lenience for mainland singing was not always favourable. He accepted his tribute when it was given him with a sudden excitement but was warned to save his treats for the performance where they might keep him from shouting his aspersions until the end of the production.

They waited together for a few minutes before being greeted once again by the director, who was certainly pleased to see the majesties, and less so to see his captains and commanders and some of his yeomanry. He denied the play's being absolutely ready. It would be well enough for one of inferior taste as the Den Asaan but ought not be acceptable to a Frewyn King, one whose noble blood was surely more refined than that of a grunting giant's despite the Den Asaan's unconquerable achievements. He bowed to the majesties, made nervous smiles, and begged them to return tomorrow for a proper showing of his opus, but the sight of so dignified a jerkin as the one on Alasdair had dazzled him and made him reconsider his refutation. As the king seemed inspired and enthused by the opera, perhaps he would allow for some errors in stage direction, some flat notes in the songs, some improvisations in the slender playbook. He was a forgiving man, and one so young for a king might betray some inexperience when speaking of Marridon's finest entertainment. Perhaps some mistakes might be gotten away with, and as any wrinkle in the performance would be smoothed for tomorrow night, he could show the play now without any fear of critique to harangue his attempts. As for the rest of the party, there was little need for him to vex himself over what a cook, a leatherworker, a blacksmith, an old woman, four captains and a wry farmer should think of his art. Fortunate he was that the writer of the playbook was at home nursing a sore throat and could therefore not repudiate the changes he had made in the lines over the last few days. As it was, the royal party might even receive a better performance than could be expected, and upon the whole he was inclined to invite them all into the theatre, knowing that there were only two of the party whose opinions truly mattered.

There was a general bustle when the royal party entered the orchestra tier of the theatre. The company murmured amongst themselves in a trepidatious hush, passing glances first to the commander and Den Asaan and then to the king and queen who were all being seated in the front row. Whispers of what was to be done and how they should act with regard to the majesties, two of such superior musical understanding, were uttered until the Frewyn Players were called out onto the stage to greet their guests accordingly. They crawled out from their caches, the men bowed and the women curtsied, and they could not but agree to performing the entire opera from the beginning for the royal party. As only the Den Asaan for an audience had been hitherto pronounced, this was a most distressing and unwelcome addition. They knew their director had no notion of the majesties' musical tutelage and refined ear, and though the Players had undergone the requisite training, they were no Marridon opera. They felt themselves only a pale imitation of what a company with many years' experience could provide. They were a comedic and dramatic troupe which borrowed its singers from the Frewyn choir, but here there would be no choir to support them. They were on their own to be judged and rated against everything they had been used to perform, but the butter biscuits in the Den Asaan's hand and the king's jerkin were enough to influence them into a more blithesome state; these were marks of the forbearance with which they ought to be treated, and the instant the director called the play to begin, they were at their places, crossing their fingers for luck and saying their prayers that no one should trip over and break the sets this time.

Tinley took his place to the left of the audience and waited for everyone to be in place to call for the lights in the house to be doused. Once there was the silence to signal everyone's preparation, the candles on the stage were lit and the orchestra began its symphony. The overture was long and grand, as the title of the opera recommended it should be, and the moment there was a lull in the stridency of music, Carrigh and Alasdair glanced at one another in grim confusion.

"This doesn't sound like it's going to be a happy tale," said Alasdair softly.

Carrigh's eyes crinkled with smile lines. "I told you, sire, that all Marridon operas end in tragedy."

"Then they might very well kill me after all."

"No, sire. You're the king. They might make you lose your sword arm, which I understand is popular in Marridon operas, having the hero lose an arm to show that no glory is obtained without sacrifice."

"I need my arms, especially my right one," said Alasdair, glancing at his limbs with chariness. "Can't they take a toe or a finger instead?"

"No one can see a finger being cut off from the balcony," Carrigh giggled.

The overture was suddenly finished, and the king and queen were obliged to be silent once more as the curtain drew up into festoons and the sconces on the back wall were lit.

The first scene to grace the stage was the prospect of a very vibrant and neat little farm, furnished with two painted cows and some pretty chickens pecking about the verdant downs. A flute played to signify the trilling of birds, a paper sun was let up behind the farmhouse, and a woman suddenly emerged from within the barn. She was small, thin, and heavy-breasted for her size, her lips were trapped in a continual pout, her blue eyes glittered with the tinge of innocence, and she sang in a shrill and trilling voice of the misfortune of being a farmer's daughter.

The commander understood from the depiction that this was meant to be an image of her life before the war, and she did her utmost not to laugh too loudly. "Well, at the very least I'm well-groomed," she snickered. "I daresay I never looked half so shining in all my life. Only painted chickens can be so forthcoming. If they knew what vicious creatures hens were, they should never have placed me beside them with bare feet."

"I think that's meant to signify your poverty," Alasdair whispered.

"Is it? Then I shall disregard the crisp shirt and handsome overalls I'm wearing."

The party laughed, making the actress on stage instantly nervous as conveyed by her inconstant notes, and they contrived to be as quiet as was possible until the intermission should arrive, if there was one to be had at all.

The first song had done, and once the fair Boudicca had finished recanting her woes of privation, the sets changed, the farm was done away, and a troupe of tenors dressed as Galleisians entered. They pillaged the farm, wheeled in cardboard fires, and began to sing of their happy destruction of Frewyn's countryside. All now seemed accurate, until two Galleisian soldiers entered with the fair Boudicca in hand and took her toward the painted Church to begin having their way with her.

Alasdair sighed and rubbed his brow. "By the Gods," he swore, gawping at the fair Boudicca singing for help as she was rived by the men.

"I do wonder," the commander said smirkingly, "how my losing my father and fighting off his assailants translated into my personal violation."

"That didn't really happen, commander," said Connors in a questioning tone.

"No, Connors. I would have remembered if it had."

Most thought it a ridiculous prospect, to have a woman singing so gaily about so horrific an atrocity, and though they laughed it off, there was one amongst the party who could not laugh at such a catastrophic display: the Den Asaan, though able to regard the skill in the sets, remark the quality of the costumes and the bearableness of the previous aria, could not condone his mate being portrayed in such a manner. Her violation by the Galleisians was not only a falsehood but it was so debase a deception as to incite his fury instantly. His eyes flared in simmering wrath. He placed his hand on his sword, nearly stood, and prepared to roar his disapprobation, but a hand on his wrist stopped him and drew his attention to the box of butter biscuits at that moment being opened. His indignation did not cease, but seeing his mate's smiling countenance while offering him a treat suggested his sitting down again. Sampling the smoothness of the chocolate and the mellifluousness of the toffee persuaded him to defer his retaliation at least until the end of the first act. With his eyes on his mate and his mind contemplating the salty sweetness of his treats, the giant was appeased, but the Frewyn Players could not be so easy, for they knew that what was to come next might be far more offensive to the Den Asaan than seeing the commander's representation abused could be.

With the unpleasantness over, fair Boudicca escaped from her captors and fled to the painted Church, but not without receiving her share of wounds. A wooden sword protruded from her side and she soon began to sing of her future as a barren and useless woman while crawling up the Church steps.

"My injury was far more gallant than that," the commander scoffed. "The violation at least would have been pleasant would it have been you, Iimon Ghaala, but to stab me when I'm already debilitated shows an inaccuracy I cannot forgive."

"But it shows how you overcame so much misfortune," said Teague, trying to suppress a smile.

"And now that they have declared me as useless with my farm and my ability to have children stricken from me, only then may I be of use to my kingdom? I joined the armed forces to avenge my father's murder and was injured saving a certain king's life. I should think that is tragedy and heroism enough for this play."

Teague simpered to himself and looked about at the rest of the party. Expressions of restrained anger, mild bemusement and aversion were all he descried in the dimmed light of the front row, excepting the Den Asaan, who though still sitting with his hand on the hilt of his blade, was inclined to give his attention to what he was eating rather than what he was watching.

Fair Boudicca then fainted and the orchestra played in the Reverend Mother who opened the door of the painted Church to find the defiled farmer at her feet. She called to have Boudicca taken inside where she was pampered to life again with song by many of the Sisters fluttering about her. Birds and woodland creatures crooned to rouse her, and when fair Boudicca sat up, she was revived with uproarious conviction. She was to go into the armed forces, she alone would save Frewyn from destruction, and the Church was whisked away to reveal a garrison littered with bare-chested men singing of the drudgery in training. Fair Boudicca wandered into the bewildering world of the army, terrified by the clash of swords and the grunts of exertion, and when she reached the conscription table was finally greeted by a handsome, straight-smiled, muscular and slender-waisted soldier who introduced himself as the Prince of Frewyn.

"I would never have done that," Alasdair protested defensively. "Vyrdin was the one who reintroduced us, and I certainly wouldn't have said hello to you if I had been undressed at the time."

Carrigh gently hushed her husband and placed the finger pointing to the half-naked tenor back into his lap.

"It would seem that the illustrator of the invitation and your darling wife have done better to dress you than the costumer has done for your counterpart," said the commander. "Would you have pageanted yourself about the garrison in such a manner, Dobhin should have plagued you even more than he already did."

Alasdair rolled his eyes and chuffed. "Well, I hope at least to have a few fantastic fights and come out just as pristine as I look there. Otherwise I'm inclined to believe that this whole play is a loss."

They had heard him. Over the din of the muted orchestra, the Players had heard the king's aspersions, and they began to worry. They looked to their director for assistance, hoping that he would reassure the royal party that the subject and content of this opera was all his idea, but Tilney did not move from his seat. The complacent smile and upright posture as he urged them to go on conveyed his pride for the piece. He showed no regard for the impropriety he might be inflicting. Even though he was incurring the royal parties' injurious looks, he maintained a wistful aspect while prompting every actor through his speeches. The more they portrayed the king as a boastful and overly valiant character, the more discomposed Alasdair grew and the happier Tilney was.

The opera endured, fair Boudicca and the shirtless prince joined the armed forces, and the closer they came to revealing their interpretation of the Den Asaan the more disconcerted and tremulous the company grew. Actors entered in fear of their lines, dreading every new song that brought his revelation still closer. Some of them even changed their speeches, much to their director's chagrin and much to their king's comfort, but the sight of the snarling beast as fair Boudicca entered the Amene garrison could not be avoided. The mask over the actor's face was misshapen and hideous, the jaw was underhung, the teeth protruded, the eyes glowed red, the falsified muscles shone a dark violet, slatternly furs screened his immense form, and the baritone voice to accompany this contrivance grumbled and garbled every word in imitation of the giant's foreign language. It was a horrendous exhibition of mistakenness and incivility, showing Rautu as a pathetic fool with a colossal sword, unable to speak Frewyn's language with any capability and forcing him to lumber about, following fair Boudicca toward the fray with all the strength the actor's legs tied to stilts could muster.

Most of the party was rapt in a silent horror, but while the commander and Alasdair laughed to themselves, Martje cackled aloud. This was all the vengeance and glorious reckoning she was desirous of seeing. All her mirth and felicity was in the notion that at last someone had seen the giant as she saw him: as an unsociable and selfish monster whose only object was to slaughter and devour everything in his path. Her hilarity was checked, however, by the odd tranquility of the Den Asaan. He had seen his counterpart — she knew he must have seen — and yet he seemed wholly disinterested. She peered over to see the butter biscuits in his lap and conceived that there must be the source of his serenity. She sighed that her revenge was halved and was content to think that she was now not alone in her perception.

Rautu was infuriated by the representation, especially when he, an Amghari and Den Asaan of Sanhedhran, had trained incessantly, had warred with Thellis his entire life, had learned every language of the mainland, and had become Den Endari at such a young age. He was a man of sense rather than elegant speeches, and he would be silent through his budding rage. The affront to him, he was aware, was the fault of the director, whom he was silently scheming to hang at the end of this performance, but the only insult that could make him stand and stop the play was one given to his mate. He had borne many horrific descriptions of himself before, and though this was by far the most erroneous, he had never seen such an ignominy of his beloved woman. Fair Boudicca could barely lift her swords, leapt about the stage as though she were afraid of the war and afraid of *him*, he whom she had defeated to coerce him into saving their kingdom's borders, and here she was a shaking, trilling dabchick, unable to do anything but force her breasts back into her armour, sing flat notes, and appear dismal and disheveled. He ate the remainder of his biscuits in teeming odium, savouring the last buttery morsels of his treats while contemplating the director's most deserved demise.

The first act was to close with Frewyn winning the Galleisian War: the stabbed and dying Galleisian soldiers pined over their defeat and the Frewyns rejoiced at Alasdair's coronation as king. Allande's death and the destruction of Westren seemed to be completely forgotten in this iteration of the kingdom's history, but the greatest inconsistency was the invitation the Den Asaan had made to the commander. The now-clothed King Alasdair asked fair Boudicca to be his queen, and while she sang her near acceptance, the monster shambled over to her and pleaded for her to return to the islands. She was struck with such a choice and could not choose between them until the Den Asaan chose for her. He took fair Boudicca into his arms and began dragging her off against her will until brave Alasdair leapt upon his horse, played by two of the lesser actors in a well-contrived suit, chased the beast to the docks, and challenged him for the right to claim fair Boudicca's hand.

"I certainly don't recall you making such a challenge," the commander laughed.

"I don't think I would be alive now if I had," said Alasdair.

The commander looked to her mate for an addition to the commentary but he could not add to her japes; his biscuits had done and so had his persistence with this piece. The empty box was crushed in his hand, his lips were taut with roused fierceness, and when the Den Asaan on stage had been defeated by King Alasdair, whose clothing had been torn off in the midst of the duel, there was the end of the giant's silence. Observing fair Boudicca fawn over the fallen creature and agree to return to the islands out of pity for his loss was the image he would retain in his mind to fuel his rage once the act should be over and his violent retribution begin.

"Did any of this really happen, commander?" Nerri asked as fair Boudicca began her woe's reprise.

"You mean did my mate force me to oblige him and steal me from an arrogant, weak and shirtless king who sings like a warbler?" The commander grinned and raised her brows. "Somewhat."

Nerri laughed with her hand covering her mouth.

"I had no idea of our king being able to sing and fight at the same time, however."

"That bit was brilliant," exclaimed Alasdair. "Only in a play will I challenge Rautu and win."

"And have your clothing vanish at the same time."

"Your king cannot defeat me," Rautu's voice rumbled.

"Oh, but he has, Iimon Ghaala," said the commander with a keen glint in her eye. "And now the poor damsel shall pity the beast who loves her. I am astonished that you have commanded yourself thus far, but your pacifiers have done and I believe your leniency with their mockery is quite over. You may trounce as you see necessary. Alasdair shall not stop you."

Alasdair agreed, and once the orchestra ceased its playing, the royal party stood from their seats to address the director. The company of actors quieted and scattered, the curtain was dropped, the members of the orchestra vanished, and Tilney was left to brook the expressions of vast discontent. The director had not stood from his seat. Instead he wondered at where everyone was going. His actors absconded, the royal party slighted; he had not expected so disastrous an outcome and could not understand the apparent outrage of Rautu, who was charging toward him with his sword raised.

The Den Asaan was entreated not to kill Tilney until he had the chance to make an apology. He obeyed and only pointed his blade at the director's neck. "You will end this," he bellowed. "Now."

"End it?" rejoined Tilney in an accent of most unanswerable dignity. "What do you mean by this outcry? We've worked ourselves tired to entertain you and this is the appreciation—" He was silenced and suddenly lifted in the air by the lapels of his fine suit. The blazing eyes of the giant throttling him made him suddenly feel that the alterations he made to the royal party's history might have been misconstrued. "I believe," said he, stammering, "I believe there has been some sort of misunderstanding."

Rautu gave him a sharp jolt to quiet his retrenching and then said in a menacing growl, "You will not perform this opera again," repeating the foreign Marridon word with pointedness. "You have dishonoured my mate, disgraced Frewyn's king, and lied to your performers and your audience. My mate came to me willingly. I asked her to be my Traala and she accepted. She did not wish to be queen and I was never defeated by the Frewyn king. I only challenge those who are worthy of my skill."

Alasdair muttered his begrudging thanks and pouted in silence.

"You will change this performance by tomorrow evening," Rautu said, tightening his grip and narrowing his gaze. "If you choose to disobey me, I will challenge you for the right to show this opera and you will lose."

"Just so everything is clear," murmured Connors to the party.

There was general laughter and then Rautu placed the director onto his feet.

Tilney was more struck with the giant's intelligence and sense of propriety than he was with the provocation he was tendered. He stared at Rautu for some time, remarking the restrained fury in his air, the taut scowl on his face, and the immense black blade in his hand. When faced with such a powerful creature, there was little else he could do than concede. "But what is to be done with the sets and the costumes?" was his only remonstrance. "And all the music that was written for the piece. What of the score and the playbook? What is to become of all of that?"

"Is there not another legend to which all these items may be contributed?" asked the commander. "I'm certain you can keep everything as is if only the title of the piece and a few names would be changed. You can even keep my name if you like. I rather enjoyed being fair and befreckled. I don't think anyone should recognize you, Alasdair, with your clothes constantly missing."

"No," mused Alasdair, "I don't think anyone would. I'll allow you to keep your opera if you make the necessary changes, but I must ask, Mr. Tilney, what in the Gods' names possessed you to make me prance about half-naked?"

Tilney shrugged. "What fond woman doesn't want to see her king bold and bare-chested?"

Carrigh's cheeks glowed with a blush, and she gave Alasdair a doting look.

All the director's faults were forgiven on Alasdair's side: his wife was giving him hints that she should like to see him half-dressed — if not completely undressed — the alterations to the play would be made, and he now could return to the keep where he could reenact all of his heroic prowess in the stage of his bedchamber with his wife's shrieks of enjoyment to applaud his efforts.

With Tilney acquitted, the actors and musicians were at liberty to return to the stage and each bowed accordingly to signify the end of their dress rehearsal. They were weary of performing for the evening, declaring it too much of a good thing, and all were happy to be better employed sitting before a fire and occupying themselves with anything but the recitation of lines.

The royal party thanked the players for their attempts, especially Mrs Cuineill who had never seen such a terrific travesty in her life. "Aye, ye young-uns made an old-un smile," she said, holding to her son's arm and shambling toward the exit. "That was somthin' else, if I tell ye. Don't really know what it was, but that was somethin' else."

They took the old woman's praise as the highest compliment; they had entertained someone at least, and if a crone from Westren can declare herself amused, they might do very well for the rest of Frewyn.

Everyone was inclined to forget the disaster as they quitted the Royal Theatre, excepting the Den Asaan, who upon reaching the double doors of the entrance stopped, turned back to Tilney, and said, "Where is your Bhendosha?"

The commander was applied to for translation and said, "I think he means the illustrator."

"For the poster or for the invitations?" asked Tilney.

Teague and Mureadh pointed out the man they believed as the illustrator, who was just fleeing the stage in horror, but were soon corrected when Tilney looked back at the stage and pointed out a small woman in the back row of performers, hiding behind half-nude Alasdair with a brush in her hand. She had been finishing the last touches on the eyes of some evil snakes for island scenes when she had been called upon to appear before the giant. She came as she was bid, but when she stood before the royal party and curtsied to the king and queen, she seemed little more than a young girl.

Rautu gave her a sideways glance. "You are the Bhendosha?"

The girl made a wide smile. "I am, Den Asaan," she said with a schoolgirl's giggle. "Mr Benleigh copied my drawing and painted it a little differently for the poster. Mr Tilney didn't like it, so I put it on the invitations to make him mad. Did you like it? I tried to make you look mean."

Rautu glowered at the girl. He took the invitation from the fold of his kilt, and holding at the end of the girl's nose said, "Does my mate resemble this woman on your summons?"

The girl looked at the commander and then at the image upon the invitation. "No. But it was supposed to look like the commander in the play, not the real one. Do you think it looks like the stage commander?"

"It does," said Alasdair eagerly. "You did very well to capture the essence of the opera, and it's you I have to thank for my new jerkin."

The girl tittered and bowed. "I like the outfits you wear to all the holiday ceremonies, Your Majesty. I was going to make your horse look like a war steed, except I was told she was a mare, and then I thought she would want to look pretty for the invitation so I gave her nice lashes and flowers for her mane."

"She looks very fine, and I'm sure she thanks you."

The girl coiled in shyness at the king's smiling answer. She bowed and hopped back to the stage that she might begin remaking the invitations to suit whatever new play they would be exhibiting.

Though Rautu still felt that the girl was in need of a reproach, the play was being changed and here he must be gratified. He had been given the opportunity to have butter biscuits for his dinner, to strangle an errant director, and to chide a young girl, and upon the whole he felt his evening was one well-spent.

The party retired to the keep for the remainder of the night, and when the morrow came, they opened their doors to see an invitation to Frewyn's first production of "Gallia and Uscen", the famous legend regarding Gallei's fair goddess and hideous patron god. They were all engaged to go for the evening, and upon seeing how well the classic tale of the golden-haired beauty and the snarling beast overtook their previous production, they gave the opera a standing ovation at its completion. Indeed the whole of Frewyn was delighted and enchanted by the performance, so much so that it kept Mad Queen Maeve from resurfacing for at least another season.

The only remembrance anyone had of the ill-fated and original opera was an order that was sent to the Larkins' masonry for a stone fountain resembling the image of the beast on the invitation. It would be a simple and rather jagged piece to carve, but its patron was willing to pay any price to have it made exactly as the card described. It was delivered it to the patron's cottage in Tyfferim and installed by Shayne at the back of the house where Martje might change the rose in the giant's mouth every other day and watch the birds bathe in the stone bowl of the Den Asaan's pleading and outstretched hand while recalling her one moment of satisfied vengeance.

*The End*

# Tales from Frewyn:
# The Reporter from Marridon

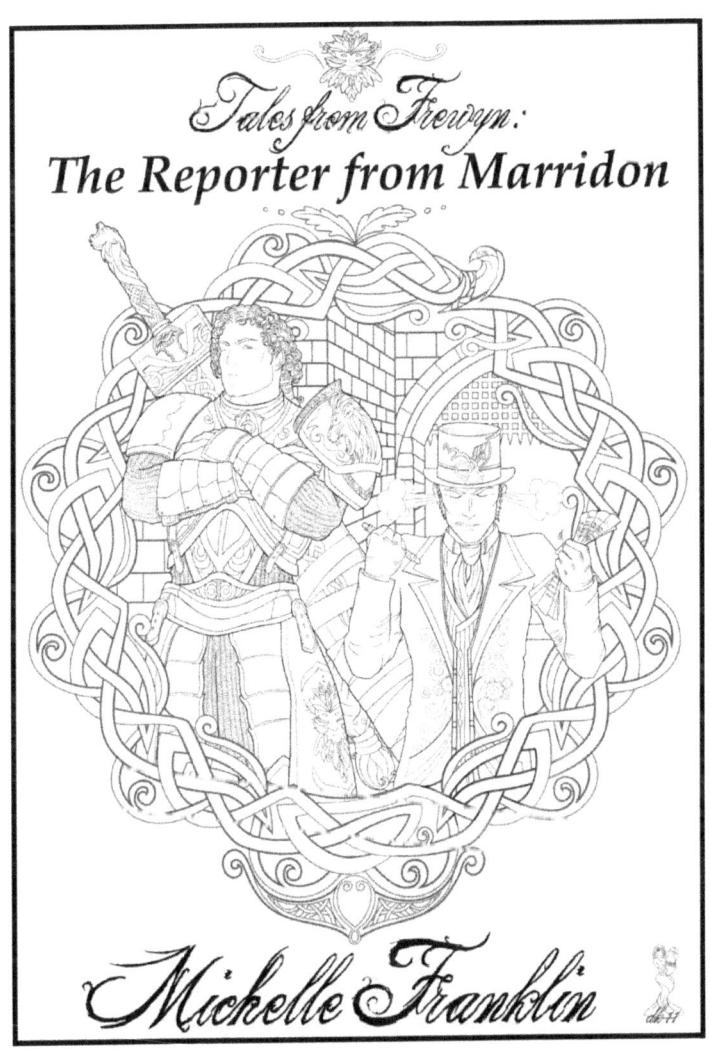

## Michelle Franklin

# Introduction

In between writing the numerous Haanta Series novels, I am known to write many short stories, most of which can be read on the Haanta Series website or can be read in the Tales from Frewyn compilations. Some of these short stories are contiguous, leading to small story arcs or even novellas. Some I end up using for the novels, some live on their own.

This story came about when someone asked me to make a character interview for a Haanta Series event. I struggled with the interview for some time and realized that I had to conduct the interview how it would have happened if a reporter had come to Frewyn looking for a story.

Featuring characters from the Haanta Series books 1-6, here is "The Reporter from Marridon." Enjoy

# CHAPTER ONE

The Duchess of Marridon's visits to Frewyn being more frequent as of late was the subject of much discussion in the Chambers. Each of her returns to the Triumvirate courts supplied fresh gossip for the officiating nobles, and the subject of the highest discussion was Her Grace's friendship with King Alasdair and her acquaintance with the commander and Den Asaan. Numerous were those who wished to know all the various beginnings of the strange connection: to be in company of a king was expected for one of the Duchess' rank and consequence, but for Her Grace to befriend a giant and a farmer was not a natural occurrence. Many became curious of the association, and when it was discovered that the woman and the giant were responsible for Frewyn's pride as a free nation, a reporter was dispatched from Marridon to their southern neighbors to obtain the particulars of the friendship's history.

The reporter, or scribe as he called himself as not to incur any censorious looks on his journey across the Dremmwel, was a small man of moderate constitution. He was thin, frail, easily agitated, but his propensity to ask questions on any and every subject endeared him to his occupation. He had little idea of whom he would be meeting when he crossed the slender reaches of the sea to the Southern Continent, but he viewed the prospect of Diras Bay with a hopeful countenance, eager to see the strange couple and even more keen to pose his prepared questions. He would be as polite as his good-breeding would allow, as he had been little used to speak to farmers, soldiers or foreigners in general. His writing was usually of a scandalous importation: imprudent marriages amongst nobles, illegitimate children, the fashion to follow in the Chambers, skilled mistresses and disconsolate wives. He had little difficulty learning all of his delicious material by bribing the various maids of the Marridon royal houses, but he had no connections in Frewyn and therefore had little notion of how to proceed there.

When the small vessel conveyed the reporter safely to the docks of the capital, he went in quest of Diras Castle, where the woman and the giant were said to reside. He was pointed the direction by the docksmaster and shown where the moneylender was at the end of the pier, that he might change his Marridon bills for Frewyn currency.

"Oh, you are generous with your assumptions, sir," said the reporter. "However, I don't mean to stay long, nor do I have the intention of bringing any commerce to your city."

The docksmaster glared at the reporter and a raised brow; that the man was from Marridon due to his niceness in dress and quickness of speech was evident, but why should he have traveled all this way with no intention of staying was an inscrutability. The docksmaster shrugged, said a dismissive, "Aye, suit yourself," and went on with his business of inspecting consignments while the reporter trotted away from the wharf.

Upon his examination of Frewyn's capital, the reporter scoffed and laughed to himself while remarking the general happenings of the early evening; Diras seemed to have no technological advancement of any sort: they were still using legs to walk, strident voices to market their wares above the general din of the marketplace, and boasted no products that promised any life-enhancing qualities. Marridon, a nation so advanced in its ideals and contrivances, to be allied with a nation with so little in the ways of machinery was a travesty — surely the Duchess was aware of their oversights. She must have pitied their lack of understanding and befriended them out of compassion rather than out of a need for their allegiance. The reporter laughed heartily to himself upon seeing the charming manner in which Frewyns still ate in taverns and hearkened the latest news from the capital square. Everything he perceived he wrote down in his journal, for this would all make a brilliant illustration of how superior Marridon was in situation. He began to receive the impression that Frewyns must not know their own ignorance, and he carried this discernment with him across the Diras Bridge and toward the front gate of the keep. Even the castle was quaint in his estimation, as it appeared to be a great deal smaller than the Chambers at Marridon, but he would save the aspersions on the keep's account until after he had seen the cheerless inside of such an ancient construct.

The reporter came to the iron gate of the castle to find a rather unbecoming guard standing in his way: a man of long face, curly and tied-back hair, immense stature and stern conviction. He seemed to be proud of his profession as a Royal Guard, marked so by the ornamental shield in his left hand, the immense sword in his right, and by the lion-head pauldron adorning his shoulder. He assumed that such a devoted creature to be brutish and uninformed, but when he demanded, "I'm here on a matter of business. You would do well to let me pass," he was treated with unexpected alacrity of mind.

"And you are, sir?" said the guard in a bemused and chary tone.

"I am a scribe from Marridon, merely here to have a consultation with two of the keep's inhabitants, to edify the people of the Triumvirate." A nod and a friendly smile would persuade the guard to open the gate, but the reporter soon found himself under a mistake to think that such behaviour would be his admittance.

The guard widened his stance and held his enormous shield in front of his chest as though preparing to strike. "Did Her Grace the Duchess of Marridon send you?" said the guard in a firm tone.

"In a manner of speaking." The reporter was still smiling.

"Then I will need to see your documentation, including your Triumvirate travel documents, Marridon identification, and Her Grace's summons to His Majesty King Alasdair Braeghan Brennin."

All the graciousness in the reporter's countenance was brooked by the guard's obdurate adherence to the law. He sighed in contempt, handed over all his certifications, and tapped his foot with impatience as each document was carefully scoured.

The guard marked the reporter's profession on his identification and instantly returned all the credentials to its owner. "None of these documents bear Her Grace's seal. Does Her Grace know that you're here?"

"She does, but that should hardly matter. I am not here to see the king."

"You are not here to see the king, sir," the guard heatedly corrected him.

The reporter fleered at such arrogance, turned aside and placed his hands on his hips. "And who might you be?" he sneered.

"I am Sir Mureadh Farhayden, Captain of the Royal Guard and appointed protector of the Brennin line, and whether you are here to appeal to His Majesty or to one of his commanders, you need the king's permission or proof of a personal summons from someone within the keep to enter. Otherwise, you may leave."

The reporter made a drawn out sigh, placing his hand over his eyes. "I'm only here to see the giant and the woman," he groaned.

Mureadh had done with this insolence. He did not care for the reporter's impropriety or his discomposed complacence. His sense of honour and duty to his commanders would make him indefatigable in his instruction, and he felt it advisable to enlighten the reporter to the positions of both persons he sought. *"And why exactly do you need to see Commander MacDaede and the Den Asaan?"*

"I'm here to carry out an interview with them—"

"Has either commander or the Den Asaan previously agreed to this interview?"

The reporter averted his eyes. "Not in so many words, but—"

Mureadh interposed with a strident laugh. "The Den Asaan would never agree to an interview or even agree to speak to someone he doesn't know."

"And how would you know that, Sir?"

"Because he is my superior officer," said Mureadh with resolution. "He trained me for the armed forces, and if there is one thing I've learned about him it is that he does not trust anyone he hasn't investigated first. He won't talk to you even if you have sent him a summons."

This was insufferable; the guard's obdurate character was bothersome and the reporter was growing weary of the debate. "And the woman?"

"The commander," Mureadh said in a meaningful accent, "would probably laugh at you for coming all this way for nothing."

The reporter swore to himself, rolled his eyes and devised a small note to be conveyed inside the keep. "Would you take this to the commander?"

"Absolutely not."

The reporter made a sly grin. "I don't believe you've read its contents." He winked and opened the note to reveal that it had been filled with more than a simple message.

Mureadh did not flinch. "Not only is bribery illegal," he said, now forgoing the formalities of title, "but those are Marridon bills. Frewyn does not accept those as currency and neither do I." He pointed the reporter back to the docks. "Leave before I carry you to the peristyle and throw you into the river."

The reporter owned himself defeated at present; he had chosen the wrong man to underestimate, and now he could only lament and be miserable. He chided himself for being precipitant in his assumptions and was forced to walk back toward the square with diminished hopes and a slighted heart. He would contrive to find another means of speaking to the woman and the giant, but for now he must find one of Frewyn's wretched taverns and search for lodgings for the coming evening.

Mureadh, rather pleased with his performance, smiled to himself and looked up to find the Den Asaan at his usual perch for this time in early evening. He had little doubt of the giant seeing the entire affair from the crenels of the castle battlements and was not surprised at the commander coming to his side a few moments later. Mureadh saluted her, he was told to be at ease, and the two of them watched the reporter scurry away from the castle entrance.

"Shall I ask about that shabby fellow?" the commander smirked.

"A reporter from Marridon, commander," Mureadh rejoined.

The commander beamed and rocked on her feet. "A reporter, indeed. You should have allowed my mate to see him." She looked up and regarded Rautu's austere watch of the capital, his trappings whipping in the gentle breeze of coming evening, his features intent and bearing low and predatory. "I daresay he would have gloried in his brilliant company," she laughed. "I'm certain Alasdair would have seen him and sent all the necessary notification to the Duchess."

"He came to see you and the Den Asaan."

The commander gave Mureadh an incredulous look. "Me? Why me? A farmer can be interesting only to those of her kind. A commander might be interesting to those in need of her assistance, but a woman can be interesting to no one at all when clothed. I should have bored him despite his inquiries, I assure you."

Mureadh simpered and shook his head, and he wondered whether he should have allowed the reporter to meet the commander and Den Asaan if only to have the former assail him with clever remarks and the latter scowl at him accordingly.

# CHAPTER TWO

ight soon came to the capital. The din of the marketplace continued in a subdued murmur, the song and raillery from the taverns became more pervasive, the dulcet scents of hardy suppers wafted from the open windows of houses, and the reporter was rapt in deliberation as to whether he should brave the horrors and joviality of a Frewyn inn or sleep within the auspices of the Church, preying upon their hospitality for a clean bed, warm food and protection from the heathens of the foreign capital. His choice, however, was made for him, as he had denied the service that the docksmaster was so good as to point out to him, and as Mureadh had kindly reminded him: only Frewyn coins would be accepted in Frewyn. There were exceptions made in the trade ports of Farriage, but as Farriage was at least three hours north by foot, he must settle for remaining in the capital.

Before resigning himself to the Church, the reporter spied two figures leaving the front gate of the castle keep. From where he stood in the square, he perceived the two leaving to be a tall man and a moderately sized woman, both of them in uniform and walking toward the marketplace presumably in quest of their evening meal. His mind for a moment was bewitched and he allowed himself to believe that these two figures were the commander and Den Asaan, but upon closer inspection he realized they were no more than a few decorated soldiers garnished with a few extra ornaments and silver and violet mantles. He thought they might be useful to him in conveying a message to the giant or his woman, and knowing now that Frewyns were too simple to understand the finer availments of currency, he decided to speak to them in a language they might better comprehend.

"Excuse me," said the reporter, addressing the two soldiers in a whimpering accent.

The man and the woman ceased their quiet conversation and turned to face the seemingly unharmed Marridonian.

"Can we help you, sir?" said the man in a sound voice.

The woman, though clad in silver armour, seemed more sympathetic to his cause, whatever it might be. "Are you injured, sir?" she said in a thick and almost indecipherable brogue.

The reporter widened his eyes and made an innocent half smile, jittering as though he were cold. "Are you officers?"

The man gave the woman a quick glance. "We are."

"Oh! Gods be praised!" the reported wailed. "Please, if you would be so kind, I have a letter that must be taken to Commander MacDaede immediately." He scribbled on a torn piece of parchment from his booklet, folded the leaf in haste and compelled it into the woman's hand.

"Can I ask what this message is for?" said the man, growing more serious in his manner.

"Something concerning her and the Den Asaan. It must be taken to her directly." The reporter sniffed and pretended to wipe a tear from his eye. "I must see her and speak with her if not both of them."

If only to be rid of the odd man from Marridon, the two agreed to do as he bid and were on their way, each of them looking over their shoulders as the pitiable creature began hobbling toward the Church. Once they were out of hearing, the two soldiers turned toward each other with penetrating looks of misgiving.

"Should I give this to the commander, Connors?" asked the woman.

"I would if only to see what all this concerns," Connors replied. "Fortunately, Nerri, we won't have to tell her to bring someone along to the meeting for protection."

Nerri and Connors exchanged a conscious laugh and walked through the lane arm in arm, shaking their heads at such an uncommon and needless occurrence.

"What a strange man. He could have just asked us to take this to the commander without the performance."

Nerri blushed and said, "I think he must have met with Mureadh at the gate." She looked down at the letter in her hand. "I wonder what he wants."

"He's a reporter," said someone from the nearby alley.

Nerri and Connors turned when they heard the familiar voice and remarked Teague removing the hood of his long cloak and slipping out of the shadows to greet them.

"Is he someone we should be concerned about?" asked Connors, narrowing his gaze to see the reporter entering the Church in the distance.

Teague shook his head. "I've been watching him since he came into the city. He's only an annoyance. Mureadh could have asked the commander to speak to him and the reporter would have been on a ship returning to Marridon by now, but Mureadh's sense of duty to our king and kingdom overpowers him sometimes."

Connors smiled to himself and thought of Teague's assertion being far too slender for describing an allegiance like Mureadh's.

"How did you know to follow him?" asked Nerri.

Teague grinned. "What well-dressed man from Marridon does not come with an escort if given the permission of the Duchess to enter the castle? Either he is a horrible spy or a foolish reporter. A spy, even a terrible one, would not ask someone else to do his work for him." He nodded toward the letter tucked in Nerri's hand. "I'll give that to the commander so that the two of you may enjoy your dinner in peace."

Teague was obliged, the letter was given him, and he said his goodevenings to the couple as they walked toward the Wayward Traveler to enjoy an excellent meal of roasted boar and braised lamb. He moved into the light to examine the contents of the letter, hung his head and sighed in humiliation for what he read, and returned to the keep in search of the commander, eager to observe her reaction to such a crudely made communication.

# CHAPTER THREE

Teague ventured up the winding stair and arrived at the entrance of the commons to find the door open and the commander sitting at the table of the main room. She was in the midst of writing her evening correspondences whereupon hearing Teague bounding up the stair, as he made no effort to mask his footfalls, she lay her quill aside and requested Teague's entrance with the easy spirits and good humour the quiet evening could provide.

"If you're in want of my company at this time of the day, I daresay you've met our visitor from Marridon," she laughed.

Teague made his bow and presented her with the letter. "I did, commander."

"Did you steal that from him or did you kindly ask him for it while holding your dagger to his neck?"

"He gave that to Nerri and Connors hoping that they would give it to you."

"Connors?" the commander scoffed. "The most dutiful and practical man in Frewyn? This reporter fellow has the very worst fortune in the world. Nerri might be pursuable on account of her being a woman, and you know how we must be sympathetic to everyone's cause.

Teague laughed behind a raised hand.

"Connors, however, is more immovable than my mate. I suppose he seems less so in comparison to Mureadh."

"He does," Teague nodded.

The commander took the message from Teague's hand, and from his half-smirk discerned that its contents promised to be a glorious horror. "Very well," she said, unfolding the letter.

"Let us see what this odious creature has to impart if only to have him removed from our kingdom."

The letter was opened, and for their dual diversion, the commander repeated the communication aloud: Come to the Diras Bridge at sunrise tomorrow. I will make the venture worth your while.

"He tried to bribe Mureadh," Teague explained.

"Ah, now I understand why he was expelled from the front gate." The commander hummed in amusement and tossed the note into the lit hearth, brightening the small fire burning within its auspices. "I know he has not been used to people cooperating with him without incentive, but assuming that everyone is corruptible shall be his demise here. Poor fellow to have chosen Mureadh as a first object."

Teague could not help but laugh when he considered the frail and fainthearted man standing before his friend's mighty form and determined countenance. He felt for the poor man, for though he was using everyone ill, had he appealed to Mureadh's piteous and charitable side he would have been safe in Marridon by morning.

"What a horrid reporter," the commander exclaimed laughingly. "Rithea could have taught him many things on the art of eavesdropping, and I daresay he could learn a few things from you about spy work. Intelligence probably does not run in his family as it does in yours. Your father could have been the most devious and designing clothier in the world, slipping messages back to Lucentia with his textile shipments and you could have been his liaison in Gallei."

Teague's eyes sparkled, and he was vastly interested in this invented position. "If I had been, I would have been more eager to convey his shipments to the annex every day."

"Perhaps you were a mere pawn in his machinations and now his sons have unknowingly overtaken his true work."

"And your father was not really a landlord and a farmer but an agent for King Dorrin somehow?"

The commander gave Teague a knowing smile. "Precisely. At least now with all of this conjecture I'll have something more interesting to tell this sorry gentleman tomorrow," she said, remarking the burnt note in the fire.

"You plan to meet with him, commander?"

"I do, and I shall be so horrid to him as to make him cry before sending him home. The Duchess would have no less for the grief he has given us. His tears will furnish her happiness, I am certain. Perhaps I can employ the orphans to empty his pockets with their heartrending faces before he goes. At least they can benefit from the money he offers so freely to others."

Teague laughed and promised to tell his brother and sister that if they should see a Marridon visitor in the Church when brought for their lessons the following morning, they must do everything in their power to extract the odd paper currency from his pockets. With great amusement to support his walk home, Teague bowed his goodnights and returned to the residential quarter to tell his mate of Frewyn's strange visitor and to remind Fionnora and Ennan of their duty for the morrow if the opportunity should arise.

# CHAPTER FOUR

hen the sun began to rise the following morning, the commander roused from her short sleep early to tend to the reporter's summons. Rautu, unused to see her dress before sunrise unless she had been up throughout the night and eager to claim his right for Khopra, asked her where she was going at such an unusual hour.

"I am going somewhere that shall promise no satisfaction on your account, Iimon Ghaala," she assured the giant.

Eager and prepared for his woman, Rautu grunted in disdain for having his morning comfort being taken from him. "I will accompany you to the gate," he purred, remarking his woman fondly.

She stood close to the giant and pressed her chest against him to incite his hunger. "And no demand for Khopra?" she said softly, her eyes twinkling.

Rautu gripped her hair by the end and coiled it around his wrist, pulling her head back and forcing her to crane her neck. "You will oblige me in the barracks when you return," was his adamant command.

The commander agreed to the arrangement, and with a few eager osculations, she was sent on her way toward the capital's natural divide with the giant certain to follow her.

Before she left the keep, however, she made a visit to the kitchen to say her hellos to Martje and Shayne, who were awake before the others in that quarter of the keep to have their breakfast together. She made herself some lemon tea in preparation for the coming arduous interrogation to follow and asked Martje if she might borrow the cup to be used as a prop or a weapon should the situation allow. She was granted her desire, and with a wish to see the cook and leatherworker later, she went to Diras Bridge to watch the brilliancy of the sun illuminate the capital.

The Church had been a favourable place for the reporter to rest: oat porridge with currants had been offered him as a supper the previous evening to guide his body into a gentle slumber, a clean bed had been found for him, prayers had been said in his name, breakfast was given at a tolerable hour, and all of this for the price of being roused before sunrise to partake in early morning services. He found the Brothers and Sisters to be a cheerful sort, eager to be of assistance and keen to help the poor and lost reporter find his way to righteousness. There was one Sister in particular of shapely figure and regular features he should have liked to have join him in his bed, and though he wished that she would have roused him from sleep with an entreaty to warm his rather cold and lonesome bed, one of the large and unbecoming Brothers came to awaken him instead. He was irked by the kindly yet unhandsome smile accorded him, but he thanked and ate and thanked again, as he knew he must if he was to be saved from the guilt-giving looks of the Reverend Mother, and was on his way before the hymns at sunrise began, before the orphans were roused and before the other children could join them for their daily lessons.

Upon leaving the Church, the reporter had found himself in a bit of luck: there, standing in the center of the Diras Bridge, was the commander. Her back was turned, a large ceramic teacup was in her hand, and she stood facing the glory of the sun's white rays, basking in the glimmering sheen of the rippling refraction of light from the waters below. She seemed heroic enough, upon his honour, but there was something wanting in her lack of heroine beauty, dearth of graceful figure or even in the confident air. He had thought that she would be taller, more striking, able to command worlds and conquer armies with the splendor of a straight smile and sharp features, but here was certainly the farmer he had heard spoken of: long unkempt hair, thick thighs, strong arms; she had a bosom enough to recommend her as a woman, but her features were so plain and undistinguished, it was a wonder to him at all what the king could have seen in her. He had heard the rumor, as had everyone of King Alasdair's once interest in the commander, but upon viewing the odd woman, the reporter was disinclined to believe any such nonsense. He whickered in astonishment for such an impossible notion and made a slow approach, riffling through his booklet for a clean leaf and taking a wrapped charcoal into his hand.

"Excuse me. Commander?" said the reporter, trying not to smirk at her appearance.

The commander spied him from the corner of her eye, sipped her tea and would not acknowledge him.

He was uncertain if this meant that she were allowing him to approach or if it meant she had plans of ignoring him, but he continued regardless of either. "I was wondering if you would do me the honour of answering a few questions?"

The commander barely smiled. "After reading your gracious note, how could I resist?"

"Then, the two soldiers did give my message to you?"

"No." She paused and took a sip of her tea. "The king's spy was the one who brought it to me."

The reporter gave a small start. "King's spy? How did he obtain my note?"

The commander made a terrible grin and kept her face firmly toward the rising sun. "I know that no one in the Chambers at Marridon is friendly with one another, but you see in this keep we are all rather like family. Once one knows something, everyone knows it. Did you really believe that your message would find its way to me unexamined?"

Though the reporter had little idea what she meant, he assumed himself fortunate that the king's spy had handed her the letter, as a herald or even a disgruntled giant were not bound by obligation to show the letter to anyone. He therefore began to make his inquiries, but the instant he opened his mouth to commence the interview, the commander interposed with:

"I despise you creatures," said she with leering condescension. "Those in your profession are ever twisting and expatiating the words of others for the interest and entertainment of your audience. You shall receive nothing useful from me, I assure you. My answers shall be long enough to supply you with a response and terse enough so that you may not fabricate a more fascinating reply." She sipped her tea and with a gesture urged him to recommence.

"Tell me how you met the Den Asaan," the reporter said, the tip of his charcoal hovering over the paper.

The commander half-smiled. "That is not a question and therefore you should have no need of an answer."

The reporter cleared his throat, felt slighted by such defensive remarks, but let it pass and moved on. "Very well. I understand you're a tactical genius of sorts—"

"Do you?" the commander rejoined. "Well then, you understand more than I ever could, for how can a woman be a genius at anything but carpet work and cookery?"

The reporter did not understand her; were she being facetious, he was left only to guess, and he therefore impressed the subject further by saying, "But I have it on the best authority that you planned the battle of the Varkne Maar."

"Then your authority is hardly the best. That was all Alasdair's plan. He is the general of our armies." She laid a hand to her breast and tossed her hair with a wistful gesture. "I am a mere commander and therefore only take orders from him."

This meeting was not advancing in the manner the reporter should have liked. Her candor and mocking assertions were distracting and every subsequent question he wished to ask was checked by her reproofs. He decided to use her own allusions to her relationship with the king to continue but expected to have little success here. "You call the king by his first name," he observed, his hand still waiting to write something down. "Are you well acquainted with his majesty?"

The commander took a sip from her cup. "I should be. We do live in the same castle."

A moment passed and there was nothing else to accompany this declaration. "Are you able to discuss your relationship?" he urged her.

"I am able to do so, yes. Shall I?" The commander shrugged and sipped her tea. She grinned when she heard an exasperated groan, and peered out from behind her cup to see the reporter struggling to write. His discomposure was all her amusement, and she snickered to herself with all the glee his growing perturbation could afford.

"I have heard," said the reporter, straining to collect himself, "that you and the king grew up together. Would you share a small part of your history by chance?"

The commander waited without considering his question, watched a school of small fish make ripples in the surface of the water below, and presently said, "No". She drank the rest of her tea and watched her antagonist writhe in frustration. "Astonishing how well my mate's tactics work," she mused, remarking the leftover tea leaves in the bottom of the cup. "Now I should not wonder why he delights in them so. They provide endless enjoyment to oneself through the boundless misery of one's adversary."

The reporter dropped his hands at his sides. "Might I ask why you're treating me this way, commander?"

"And I might ask why with so little propriety you decided to bribe my mate's first officer, accost two of my commanders, and disturb our peace," she said firmly, finally turning to him.

The reporter shrank under the commander's even stare. Though her person was approachable and her character wry, there was a fierceness to her that when provoked was unmistakable. He saw now his error in judging her as one of Frewyn's shy yeomanry and realized she agreed to this meeting for retaliation. He would ask one last question and then he would be done. "Can you tell me anything about the Den Asaan?" Where he had expected another curt reply, his question was received with graciousness.

The commander's usual air restored, and with folded arms and a cocked hip, she said, "I can tell you a multitude of things. What exactly do you want to know?"

By this time, the reporter's spirits were so wearied that he had little notion of what he should ask first. He considered names, observances, cultural differences, but his primary consideration was, "The Duchess has mentioned the Haanta ritual of Khopra on occasion when her visitor from Mharvholan is in Marridon. Have you performed this ritual with the Den Asaan?"

"I daresay you don't know what the ritual entails, for if you did, you would not have asked that question." The commander laughed at the reporter's mistake, wiped mirthful tears from her eyes and shook her head. "If you will be good and wait here a moment, I shall bring someone to answer that question in the manner it should be answered."

The reporter watched her walk from the bridge to the castle gate, make a small gesture with her hand, and from the high battlements of the keep leapt down a menacing-looking creature of stern face, immense stature, and fur-clad form. She spoke a few words to the giant, motioned toward himself, and began leading the hulking beast to his place at the bridge. He heard the thunder of the approaching steps, observed the sheen of the tremendous black blade at the giant's side, and acknowledged that this monstrosity must be the Den Asaan.

Now that he had seen the one he was most desirous of questioning, however, he knew not how he could have convinced himself to speak to the moving mountain without the commander's comforting presence.

# Chapter Five

The reporter groveled in terror when the giant was standing before him: arms built, features austere, a sword so gargantuan, a trove of trappings so varied and astounding as he had never before seen. The giant's black and violet eyes and intimidating glare were enough to silence him, and though he wished to abscond and hide behind a nearby tree, his notions could not govern his frozen legs.

The commander held out her hand and the giant made a curt bow without lowering his eyes. "I would like you to meet my mate. Here is the affable Den Asaan Rautu, prepared to answer all of your inquiries with smiling agreement." She paused and heard a few whimpers from the shivering reporter. "What? Have you nothing to ask? A moment ago you were brimming with questions. I believe you asked about Khopra. My mate shall be happy to illuminate your understanding."

"Come, woman," the giant bellowed. "We will give him a demonstration."

The reporter was agape with horror: to hear a woman so addressed was deplorable, but to see the beast turning one who was supposedly his beloved wife around and forcing her to bend over the railing of the bridge while pressing his lower region against her backside was unforgiveable. He closed his eyes with one hand and waved the other about in a fever of agitation. "I understand you! I understand you perfectly! No need to show me," he shrieked.

The giant, too rapt in the prospect of his mate's warm thighs, ignored the man's entreaties and began removing his kilt when the commander interrupted him.

"While I should relish a public display, especially while in view of the Church," she said, righting herself, "I don't believe it prudent to show the flocking children such a bestial custom." She pointed to the children beginning to gather in the churchyard.

"Hmph," was all the giant's reply, and he reluctantly backed away from his mate, considering the enjoyment he would be having later.

"I believe you understand the ritual now," the commander said to the reporter. "The request is made, consent is given and Khopra is had."

"Yes, yes. I understand you perfectly." The reporter fumbled with his charcoal and wiped the sweat from his brow with the back of his hand. "I was made to understand that you enjoy chocolate Den Asaan," he said nervously. "Ever since the Triumvirate Chocolate Company has opened a branch in Frewyn, its revenue has tripled, many believe due to your contribution alone."

Rautu stared at the reporter. He waited for a question but there was none to follow. "And?"

"And you seem to consume more chocolate in a month than all of Marridon does in a year."

"And?"

"And how do you account for this odd diet?"

Rautu's eyes flared at the accusation. "I train recruits and condition my form for most of the day. I eat my meals with my mate, and when I am hungry, I eat what is available until I am able to hunt when training for the day is done."

"Or," the commander said, "until I'm free from my daily orders so that I may continue my duties to him as cook, chocolate is his food of choice when he has already eaten all the meat in the larder."

Growing calmer and more sagacious, the reporter reached into his pocket and produced a small bar wrapped in foil.

"Then I was not wrong in bringing you this," he said offering it to the giant.

Rautu observed the small gift with a chary eye. He inspected its shape and thickness and could be under no mistake as to what it was due to the subject under discussion. His only question now was what kind of chocolate was within the foil. Were it a dark chocolate, he should be pleased at such tribute; were it semisweet, it could be deemed as tolerable; were it milk chocolate or some variation of such with nuts, it could only be considered mildly acceptable; and were it the abominable white chocolate or something tainted by fruit, such objectionable effrontery would warrant the giver an expulsion from the capital. He must catch its scent to know what it was, and though his sense of smell was exceptional, he could not exhibit his powers through a blockade of foil. He must accept it, he must take it into his hand, and he must peel back the wrapping to establish its worthiness.

A look, a scent, and the giant's countenance grew livid: within the folds of the silver foil, he noted a white colour, and in a mistake of aspiration that perhaps he was only seeing the end of one piece, Rautu tore open the remaining foil to find a bar of solid white chocolate decorated with dried fruits. The white chocolate was horror enough, but that it should be laden with fruit was unforgiveable. The offense was too great, and something must be done. Only being ejected from the capital for such a slight would sate the giant's anger, and to prove his infuriation, the Den Asaan threw the chocolate in the river, grabbed the reporter by the collar of his shirt and roared at his prey.

"Your presence has been tolerated long enough," he said in a dreadful wrawl.

He stormed along the Diras River with the whimpering man dangling from his clasp and did not stop until they reached the docks. A trade ship bound for Marridon was being prepared for leave and the Den Asaan notified the docksmaster of there being a new passenger aboard.

"Gihondenri," Rautu seethed, addressing the docksmaster, "this man does not leave this ship until it has docked in Marridon." He displayed his prey for the docksmaster to examine and then hurled him across the wharf and onto the deck of the trade vessel, where he landed upon a pile of wheat sacks and did not dare right himself until the giant was gone.

Rautu thundered back to the castle while the commander made all the arrangements for a letter to be sent with the trade ship to the Duchess, thanking her for providing some entertainment for her mate and asking her to send another just like him for a future time. She passed the note along to the ship's captain, and before leaving the wharf, she decided to give the toppled reporter one last piece of advice:

"The easiest way to tame a giant is to feed it when it is hungry, and the easiest way to anger it is to feed it something it does not like." She turned and began walking down the steps of the pier. "Give my compliments to my friend the Duchess and do not return to Frewyn without hers to merit your visit," she called out as the ship was beginning to take sail.

As the vessel steered out of Diras Bay, morning had arrived in the Frewyn capital. Trade at the docks renewed, shoppes and stalls in the marketplace were opened, and the kingdom's main city was aglow with life. The reporter recollected himself just in time to hear the peal of the church bell calling Frewyn children to school and to see guards at the port changing for their morning patrol. Although the reporter had met with almost every personage of consequence in the Frewyn capital excepting the king, his visit had yielded little result: being rejected at the castle gate, sleeping in a stale Church, being forced to humble himself before two common commanders, being terrified and nearly mauled by a ferocious giant, suffering the snickering remarks of a complacent woman; these occurrences were all excellent for a novelist, but for a reporter in want of a story, they could afford no material worthy of print.

# About the Author

Michelle Franklin is a small woman of moderate consequence who writes many, many books about giants, romance, and chocolate. You can find more about her and the Haanta series at her website: http://thehaanta.blogspot.ca/